Mrs. Piccolo's Easy Chair

A RICHARD JACKSON BOOK

Mrs. Piccolo's Easy Chair

story by JEAN JACKSON • pictures by DIANE GREENSEID

A DK INK BOOK • DK PUBLISHING, INC.

A Richard Jackson Book

DK Publishing, Inc., 95 Madison Avenue, New York, New York 10016
Visit us on the World Wide Web at http://www.dk.com

Library of Congress Cataloging-in-Publication Data
Jackson, Jean.
Mrs. Piccolo's easy chair / by Jean Jackson; illustrated by Diane Greenseid.—1st. ed.
p. cm.
Summary: Hungry for a snack, Mrs. Piccolo's easy chair follows her to the grocery store,
swallowing up several people as it goes.
ISBN 0-7894-2580-7
[1. Chairs—Fiction. 2. Supermarkets—Fiction.] I. Greenseid, Diane, ill. II. Title.
PZ7.J136225Mr 1999 [E]—dc21 98-22782 CIP AC

Book design by Jennifer Browne.
The illustrations for this book were painted in acrylic.
The text of this book is set in 19 point Weiss.
Printed and bound in U.S.A.

First Edition, 1999
2 4 6 8 10 9 7 5 3 1

In memory of my father, Ralph Candiotti

—J.J.

To Jane with love

—D.G.

Mrs. Piccolo was a small woman. When she sat in her favorite easy chair she was nearly swallowed up, and sometimes she had trouble extracting herself from its cushiony clutches.

"Let me go, chair," she would say. "I have things to do and places to be!" And then, if the chair was in a generous mood, it would burp and Mrs. Piccolo would pop out like a watermelon seed.

But if the chair was not in a generous mood, it would make itself as soft and billowy as a summer cloud and then, no matter how much Mrs. Piccolo kicked her tiny legs and waved her thin arms, she could not get free. The chair would let Mrs. Piccolo go only if she promised to get it a snack.

The chair loved snacks. Its favorite was cheese puffs—it always kept a few hidden under its cushion.

One morning Mrs. Piccolo was getting ready to go to the grocery store. She put on some pink lipstick, high-heeled shoes, and a tiny yellow hat with a bee on top. Then off she went, never dreaming that the chair, which had a sudden craving for cheese puffs, had decided to follow her.

The chair peeked out the door until it saw Mrs. Piccolo walk down the hill and turn the corner. Then it hurried after her.

An old man sitting on his front porch stood up and said, "I say, isn't that an easy chair passing by?"

"Mind your own business," the chair called over its shoulder.

"I say," said the old man, sitting back down. "And it talks, too!"

The chair rounded the corner just in
time to see Mrs. Piccolo pass through
the automatic doors of Friendly Fred's
Fine Foods. The chair closed its eyes.
It could just see them—rows and
rows of crunchy orange
cheese puffs. . . .

"What are you doing?" A deep, growly voice startled the chair from its daydream.

"Where are you going?" the voice asked. "Let me see your license. What? You don't have a license? We can't have easy chairs strolling down the streets without a license. I shall have to arrest you."

The chair did not want to be arrested. It stretched out a little and fluffed up its cushions and made itself so inviting that the police officer couldn't help himself—he just had to sit a minute and rest his tired feet. As soon as the officer sat down, *slurp-gulp*, the chair swallowed him up. Then, feeling a mite heavier, it walked up to the front door of Friendly Fred's Fine Foods.

When Friendly Fred saw an easy chair trying to squeeze through his front door, he rushed over. "Can't you read?" he said, pointing to a sign on the door. "No easy chairs!"

"Why, that's a silly rule," the chair said. "What do you have against easy chairs?"

"I have nothing against easy chairs when they're sitting at home in their living rooms," said Friendly Fred. "But when they come into my store they hog the aisles and bump into displays and spill oranges all over the floor. And they always always *always* sit in front of my cheese-puff rack and drool."

"I never drool," said the easy chair, highly insulted.

"What a mess they make!" Friendly Fred continued. "I have to call for a bucket and mop on aisle three. It's always aisle three— the cheese-puff aisle!"

The easy chair snorted. Then it stuck out its leg and tripped Friendly Fred. He fell into the chair and then, *slurp-gulp,* the chair swallowed him up.

Clickety-clack-clickety-clack, the chair skipped on down the aisle to the snack-foods section. It shook itself until all the coins that had ever fallen between the cracks of its cushions clattered to the floor. There was enough to buy three jumbo bags of cheese puffs!

The easy chair hurried to the checkout. It wanted to be home before

Mrs. Piccolo. But as soon as it got in line, Mrs. Piccolo rounded the frozen-food aisle and headed straight toward it! Luckily a tomato fell out of her cart, and as she bent to pick it up, the chair hid behind a very large woman wearing a big yellow wig. Two plump boys were clinging to her dress. When they saw the chair they immediately climbed into it and began to jump.

"Oooof!" said the police officer.

"Aaaarf!" said Friendly Fred.

"Wheeeee!" said the two boys.

"I am not a trampoline," said the chair. "If you don't get off me at once, I'll swallow you up!"

The boys jumped even higher. "So swallow us up!" they said. And *slurp-gulp, slurp-gulp,* that is just what the chair did.

When the very large woman saw her sons disappear into the cushions of an overstuffed easy chair, she let go of her cart and dived in after them. "Ugh!" said the chair. Then, *slurp-gulp,* it swallowed her up, too.

The chair paid for its cheese puffs and waddled out the door. It was so heavy every step was a struggle. The hill home seemed *way* steeper than before. Just as the chair reached the gate in front of Mrs. Piccolo's house,

it felt a bubble growing inside its stomach, getting bigger and bigger and bigger until the chair couldn't help itself, and with a loud burp, it expelled the police officer, the grocer, and the very large woman and her two plump boys.

Just then Mrs. Piccolo appeared with her bag of groceries. "What in the world is going on?" she asked. "How did my easy chair get out here on the sidewalk?"

"It ate us up!" said one of the plump boys.

"Gobble-gobble, slurp-slurp!" said the other.

The adults cleared their throats and shuffled their feet. They were too embarrassed to admit that they had been swallowed up by an old woman's easy chair.

The police officer and Friendly Fred carried the easy chair back to its corner in Mrs. Piccolo's living room. Then Mrs. Piccolo served everyone warm brownies and cold punch. A muffled crunching came from the corner of the living room—the chair had opened one of its bags of cheese puffs.

"The chair's making noises," said one of the boys.

"It's eating," whispered the other.

Their mother stood up. "We really must be going," she said. "Thank you for the lovely snack."

"Yes, thank you, thank you," said Friendly Fred and the police officer. "We have to get back to work now."

Mrs. Piccolo said good-bye to her surprise guests. Then she returned to the living room and plopped down in the easy chair.

"I don't know what got into you, following me to the grocery store and then swallowing up all those nice people," she said. "What do you have to say for yourself?"

The chair made a little burp, and a cheese puff flew out from between its cushions and bounced on the floor. Mrs. Piccolo giggled and the easy chair smiled, and in the lazy warmth of the afternoon sun they yawned, stretched, and closed their eyes. It was *way* past naptime.